The Rabbit's Red Handkerchief

DAYOUNG YUN 지음

BOOKK✎

Author's Note

I would like to let you know that this is a book for men and women of all ages because the hero of this fairy tale book is modelled after the little rabbit. So, the author's intention is to reach out to readers friendly by using the rabbit who possesses cuteness. Moreover, this book is both entertaining and instructive. I hope you to experience a rewarding day by giving someone a helping hand.

If you come to know about that,
you would be able to be
better than before.

Once upon a time, a little rabbit lived in an apple tree hole, which was located in a deep ravine that was colorful mushrooms in front of the hole.

One day, after school, the little rabbit started
thinking a lot about a rewarding experience
because she received a task that should write
a diary related to a meaningful day
from her teacher.

But, she didn't have the experience that she was able to feel rewarded. While she worried and thought about her task, her mother hid out of sight and then secretly watched her daughter who seemed to have some worries about something.

So, her mother called the rabbit who was immersed in thought and handed her a red handkerchief, with saying some encouraging and hearty words to her. "Baby, receive this red handkerchief. It will bring happiness to you and should be helpful. Cheer up!" she said, "Thanks mom." The little rabbit was given it by her and left home.

However, she had another weight on her mind. That was how she use it.

She tried wearing the scarf around her neck and covering her face by using it.

During worrying about how to use it, the sky was covered all over with dark clouds. It seemed as if it was going to rain. Finally, she decided to wear a scarf around her neck. Then she started seeing herself mirrored in the water.

What's even worse, it began to rain.
The more dark clouds gathered overhead,
the more it was pouring with rain. During raining,
she was sitting in front of the water in the pouring
rain, crying loudly. However, she came to listen to
the sound of a crying baby frog.

Then I'll help you !

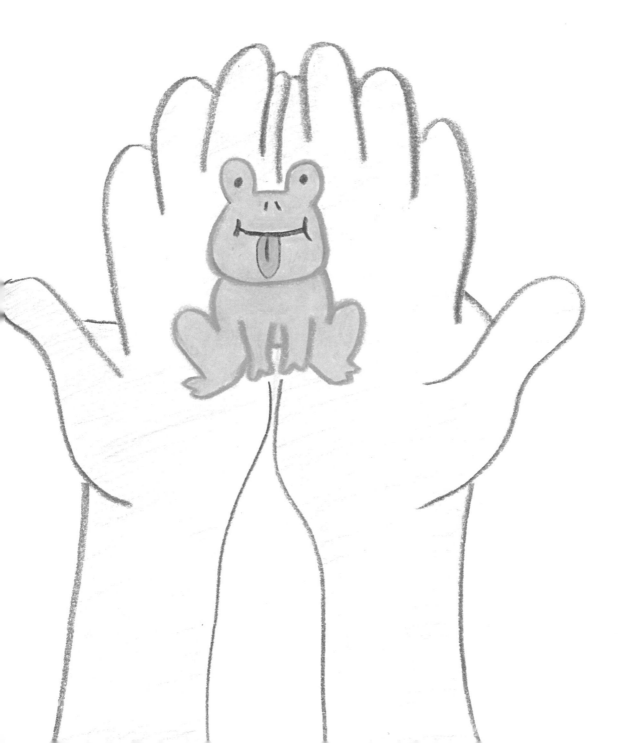

She brought the friend a small pond that was in front of her. The frog was left on a lotus leaf by her. They took shelter from the rain under her red handkerchief.

As the time goes on, the heavy rain stopped. After they waited until rain stopped, the sun was shining in the clear sky. The rabbit and her friend, the baby frog, said goodbye to each other and said we would be able to see each other again from time out of mind on the street.

The two split up and went their separate ways.

On her way home, the rabbit heard a rustle
through the bushes and noticed where the
rustle sound was coming from.

And then, she found the spot where the sound was making. The rabbit was surprised because of a baby squirrel who was crying in front of lots of nuts, such as chestnuts and acorns.

"Hey, what's wrong with you?
Why are you crying?", said the rabbit.
The squirrel said, "Before the winter comes,
I have to keep gathering lots of nuts as much as
possible. I tried to have chestnuts and acorns in
my mouth as much as possible. Although I
gathered them at most, there still remain these
nuts. I want to take them home."

"What should I do?"

Then I'll help you !

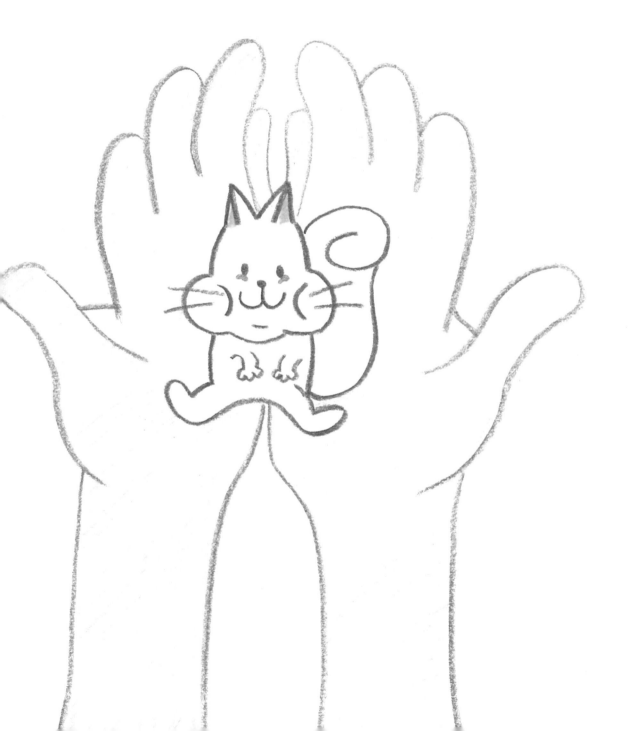

The rabbit was ready to put them in her handkerchief that was given by her mother in order to help the second friend bring them to his home. The squirrel's face was glowing with a smile because his worry was able to be solved to some extent.

After they finished bringing them into the red
handkerchief, the rabbit decided to take him
to his home.

The baby squirrel thanked her for helping him,
hanging from a bough with a smile.
They said goodbye to each other.

The rabbit became much more happier than before
because she could give the baby frog and the squirrel
a helping hand by using only this red handkerchief.
Due to these reasons, she whistled and sang
snatches of songs.

While she was humming songs to herself, she could suddenly hear the sound of splashing in the river.

So, she looked across to see where the sound was
coming from.
It turned out that there were crying two beavers who
were mother-son relationship.

The rabbit wondered why they were crying.
So, she asked why they were sad and
why they had to take hands.

And then they said with the deeply thinking.
"We have to take hands in order to prevent
us from sweeping away in the strong current
due to the heavy rain. But, we couldn't do
that because the current was swift.
What should we do?"

After she listened to all of their stories, she was thinking about their worries. And then she decided to help them as much as she could.

Then I'll help you !

The rabbit started being busy tying their hands
together with her red handkerchief.

Then they could come to hold each other's
hands and thank to her.

The little rabbit has spent a day in doing good.
She acted her part well by doing good.
As she was not far from her house, her mother
had came out to get a side street near home.

She run to her mother and kissed her on the cheek.
Then her mother kept holding tightly.

After the baby was in its mother's arms,
her mother noticed why her daughter didn't
have the red handkerchief that she gave her
in this morning.

The little rabbit started explaining her to
what she did good for a day and why she
didn't have the red handkerchief now.

As listening to her all of her stories, her mother commended highly by stroking her hand and added some words, "So, how was your day? You went through more trouble for today than anyone else. I'm so happy because I think that I could help you solve your worry. It was so praiseworthy that you could give someone a helping hand."

"I'm proud of you !
You did great."

At that time when the little rabbit arrived at home, the three friends who were helped from her whenever they had a difficulty in being endangered started being ready to separately make a gift for her .

The first friend, the baby frog, made her up a bouquet by using a lotus flower that was in bloom on a pond in order to thank her for helping him escape from the overflowing pond.

The baby squirrel who she met for the second time was mixing flour, eggs, and sugar to make a cake in order to bake a cake for her. The cake was made of a number of chestnuts and acorns with the blueberry flavored whipped cream.

Lastly, two beavers who were the mother-son relationship were making a necklace set with pearls by tying the shells together. Also, the baby beaver who was sitting next to his mother was picking up a shell on the bottom and playing with it well.

The rabbit who was in the house had taking supper with her mother. During the meal time, someone was pressing to doorbell.

So , she called , with saying
"Who are you ?", but no one answered .
Then she tried the door.

By the way, to her surprise it opened and came to
look upon the scene before her.
There were two friends who said "Hi!" to her
in front of the door.

The reason why she was surprised was that friends who were helped by her were waiting for her in front of the rabbit's house, with preparing for some gifts that were going to give her. The baby beaver waved the red handkerchief to her.

The rabbit began to reach out to her friends and then blew out a candle on the cake. She was also putting a lotus flower in her ear and wearing a necklace that beavers made by using pearls and shells.
And, they enjoyed having a party.

After the party was over, the rabbit was ready
to write a diary, which was given as a task from
her teacher. At first she looked worried because
what to write about a rewarding experience, but
now she was sure that there was much more to be
written about a meaningful day than before.

Because she thought so, she became happy.
Also, she was holding her red handkerchief
when she wrote a diary.

Her diary was written like this.

Sat. June. 24th

Today I've had a product-ive and meaningful day by helping my friends. I'd like to thank my mom for giving me the red handkerd

While she wrote her diary, she started falling asleep in her seat, with nodding her head and had a terrible dream.

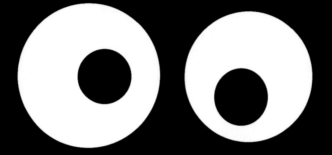

In her dream, there was her mother who was
in danger, tying to a tree.
She seemed to be distressed due to hanging
upside-down from the tree.

While the little rabbit flopped down on the bottom and wept sadly because of her mother who was in danger, the red handkerchief was in her dream and offered to give her assistance, with patting her on the shoulder. And he said,
"Hey, I'll help you. Don't worry about that."

"From now on, you're going to be changed differently. So, please close your eyes and count to ten in your mind."

Shortly after his encouragement and his magic,
her body turned into a caterpillar.
The handkerchief said, "Your changed body will
be able to help you when you save your mother.
You can do it ! Use your brain."

"And believe yourself that you can do it ."

She was surprised because she found herself changed differently. Also, she was greatly emboldened by his words of encouragement.

After being changed, she approached
her mother who was tied to the tree and
cut a rope that tying to her mother by
using her front teeth. And then her
mother who was tied to the tree came
to fall to the ground.

The little rabbit was ready to receive falling her mother by using her red handkerchief as soon as her mother fell to the bottom. Finally, she did it !

After she saved her mother from the threat, they kept embracing each other and then wept for joy at the sight of her mother who was safely rescued. The baby rabbit forced herself to calm down and gave her mother a big hug.

The rabbit who slept deeply during writing
her diary woke with a snotty nose.
In other words, her face was all covered with
tears and nasal discharge. Also, she was holding
her red handkerchief amid the hustle and bustle.

After she was wide awake, she was rubbing
her eyes and wiping her nose. At that time when
she did that, her mother came close and cradled
her daughter in her arms.
The baby was aware that she had the dream.
As she got a great relief, she had a good cry.

The little rabbit left word behind like that.
"Thanks, mom and the red handkerchief.
Thanks to you all, I could feel rewarded today.
I love you all. ♥"

Before she went to bed early, she hung up her red
handkerchief on the hook in the wall. And then ,
she crawled into a comfortable bed and began to sleep.
She thought that she had great time by helping
others on her own although she had a terrible dream.
She could have spent her time more profitably
by being of good behavior .

Have you ever had a productive day ?
Or have you ever been praiseworthy ?
If not, why don' t you look around for people
around you and reach out to give a helping
hand from now on ?

The Rabbit's Red Handkerchief

발 행 | 2017년 03월 22일

저 자 | DAYOUNG YUN

펴낸이 | 한건희

펴낸곳 | 주식회사 부크크

출판등록 | 2014.07.15.(제2014-16호)

주 소 | 경기도 부천시 원미구 춘의동 202 춘의테크노파크2단지 202동 1306호

전 화 | (070) 4085-7599

이메일 | info@bookk.co.kr

ISBN | 979-11-272-1349-7

www.bookk.co.kr